The Flying Acorns

by JAMES STEVENSON

GREENWILLOW BOOKS, New York

Watercolor paints and a black pen were used for the full-color art.
The text was hand-lettered by the author.
Copyright © 1993 by James Stevenson. All rights reserved. No part of this book
may be reproduced or utilized in any form or by any means, electronic or mechanical,
including photocopying, recording, or by any information storage and retrieval system,
without permission in writing from the Publisher, Greenwillow Books, a division
of William Morrow & Company, Inc., 1350 Avenue of the Americas, New York, NY 10019.
Printed in Hong Kong by South China Printing Company (1988) Ltd.
First Edition   10 9 8 7 6 5 4 3 2 1

Library of Congress Cataloging-in-Publication Data
Stevenson, James (date)
The flying acorns / by James Stevenson.
p.   cm.
Summary: Three squirrels looking for excitement
in their lives try to pull together an acrobatics act
for the circus that is coming to their part of the forest.
ISBN 0-688-11418-0. ISBN 0-688-11419-9 (lib.)
[1. Acrobats—Fiction.   2. Squirrels—Fiction.]
I. Title.   PZ7.S84748FI   1993
[E]—dc20   91-45678   CIP   AC